'The inspe[...] ordered that the bird be searched. One of the agents stalled saying it made him feel sick, and after some fierce pecking another withdrew sucking a bleeding finger'

ITALO CALVINO
Born 15 October 1923, Havana, Cuba
Died 19 September 1985, Siena, Italy

'The Queen's Necklace' and 'The Workshop Hen' were
written in Italian and first published in 1993. They were
translated into English and published in *Numbers in the Dark*
in 1996.

ALSO PUBLISHED BY PENGUIN BOOKS
The Path to the Spiders' Nest · *Italian Folktales* · *The Complete
Cosmicomics* · *Under the Jaguar Sun* · *Six Memos for the Next
Millennium* · *Why Read the Classics?* · *Numbers in the Dark and
Other Stories* · *Hermit in Paris* · *The Road to San Giovanni*

ITALO CALVINO

The Queen's Necklace

TRANSLATED BY TIM PARKS

PENGUIN BOOKS

PENGUIN CLASSICS

Published by the Penguin Group
Penguin Books Ltd, 80 Strand, London WC2R ORL, England
Penguin Group (USA) Inc., 375 Hudson Street, New York, New York 10014, USA
Penguin Group (Canada), 90 Eglinton Avenue East, Suite 700, Toronto, Ontario,
Canada M4P 2Y3 (a division of Pearson Penguin Canada Inc.)
Penguin Ireland, 25 St Stephen's Green, Dublin 2, Ireland (a division of Penguin Books Ltd)
Penguin Group (Australia), 250 Camberwell Road, Camberwell, Victoria 3124, Australia
(a division of Pearson Australia Group Pty Ltd)
Penguin Books India Pvt Ltd, 11 Community Centre, Panchsheel Park,
New Delhi – 110 017, India
Penguin Group (NZ), 67 Apollo Drive, Rosedale, North Shore 0632, New Zealand
(a division of Pearson New Zealand Ltd)
Penguin Books (South Africa) (Pty) Ltd, 24 Sturdee Avenue, Rosebank, Johannesburg 2196,
South Africa

Penguin Books Ltd, Registered Offices: 80 Strand, London WC2R ORL, England

www.penguin.com

Selected from *Numbers in the Dark and Other Stories* published by Penguin Books 2009
This edition published in Penguin Classics 2011
1

Typeset by Jouve (UK), Milton Keynes
Printed in England by Clays Ltd, St Ives plc

ISBN: 978-0-141-19583-4

www.greenpenguin.co.uk

Penguin Books is committed to a sustainable future
for our business, our readers and our planet.
The book in your hands is made from paper
certified by the Forest Stewardship Council.

Contents

The Queen's Necklace

Pietro and Tommaso were always arguing.

At dawn the squeaking of their old bicycles and the sound of their voices – Pietro's hollow and nasal, Tommaso's husky and sometimes hoarse – were the only noises to be heard in the empty streets. They used to cycle together to the factory where they worked. From the other side of the shutter slats you could still feel the sleep and the darkness weighing on the rooms. The muffled ringing of alarm clocks began a sporadic dialogue from one house to the next, becoming denser in the suburbs, until finally it merged, as town merged into country, into a back and forth of cock-a-doodle-doos.

Busy as they were arguing at the tops of their voices, the two workers didn't notice this first stirring of daily sounds: anyway they were both deaf; Pietro had been a little hard of hearing for some years now, while Tommaso had a constant whistle in one ear that went back to the First World War.

'That's how things are, old friend,' Pietro, a big fellow of sixty-odd, uncertainly balanced on his wobbling machine, thundered down at Tommaso, five years his elder, but smaller and already somewhat bent. 'You've lost faith, old friend. I know myself that with the way things are today having kids means going hungry, but tomorrow you never know, you never know which side the scales might come down, tomorrow having kids could mean wealth. That's how I see things, and rightly so.'

Without taking his eyes off his friend, yellow bulbs opening wide, Tommaso let out sharp cries that would suddenly turn hoarse: 'Ye-ess, ye-ess! What's got to be said to a worker starting a family is this!: bringing babies into the world you're only adding to poverty and unemployment! That's what! That's what he's got to know! I'm telling you. I've said it before and I'll say it again!'

Their discussion this morning was on the general question, does an increase in the population favour or damage the workers? Pietro was optimistic and Tommaso pessimistic. Behind this conflict of views lay the marriage planned between Pietro's son and Tommaso's daughter. Pietro was for it and Tommaso against.

'And anyway, they haven't had kids yet!' Pietro suddenly came back. 'All in good time! That's all we need! We're talking about an engagement, not about kids!'

Tommaso yelled: 'When people marry, they have kids!'

'In the country! Where you were born!' Pietro came back. He almost got his wheel caught in a tram rail. He swore.

'Wha-aat?' Tommaso shouted, pedalling ahead.

Pietro shook his head and said nothing. They went on in silence for a while.

'Then, of course,' Pietro said, winding up a train of thought out loud, 'when they come, they come!'

They had left the city behind them and were riding along a raised road between fields left fallow. There were some last patches of fog. Above a grey horizon not far away loomed the factory.

An engine droned behind them; they had just got themselves on the verge when a big smart car went by.

The road wasn't tarred, the dust the car lifted cloaked the two cyclists and from the thick cloud came Tommaso's raised voice: 'And it's in the exclusive interest o-of . . . oh, oh, oh!' The dust he'd swallowed brought on a fit of coughing and his short arm emerged from the cloud and pointed in the direction of the car, doubtless to suggest the interest of the ruling classes. Pietro, trying to speak while coughing from a red face, said: 'Uugh . . . Not . . . uugh . . . for . . . uugh . . . lo-ong,'

3

pointing at the car with a decidedly negative gesture to express the idea that the future did not belong to the owners of custom-built automobiles.

The car was racing away when one of its doors came open. A hand thrust it wide so that it banged back and a woman in silhouette almost threw herself out. But whoever was driving braked at once; the woman jumped down, and in the thin morning mist the workers saw her run across the road. She had blonde hair, a long black dress and a cape of blue fox furs, their tails in fringes.

A man wearing an overcoat got out of the car, shouting: 'You're crazy! You're crazy!' The woman was already dashing away from the road through the bushes, and the man set off after her until they both disappeared.

Below the road were meadows with dense thickets of shrubs, and the two workers saw the woman appearing and disappearing in and out of them, her steps short and quick in the heavy dew. With one hand she held her skirt from touching the ground and she jerked her shoulders to free herself from the branches that caught at her fox tails. She even began to bend the branches so that they would spring back on the man who was chasing her, though without really hurrying and without, it seemed, too much desire to catch her. The woman ran wild in the meadows, shrieked with laughter, shook the dew on the branches down on to her hair. Until he,

4

calm as ever, instead of following her, cut her off and took her by the elbows; and it looked as though she was wriggling to escape and biting him.

The two workers followed the chase from the raised road, though they never stopped pedalling or paying attention to where they were going. They watched silently, eyebrows raised and mouths open, with a gravity more diffident than curious. They were almost up to the stationary car, left there with its doors open, when the man in the overcoat came back, holding the woman who was forcing him to push her along and yelling almost like a child. They shut themselves in the car and set off; and again the cyclists ran into the dust.

'While we're starting our day,' choked Tommaso, 'the drunkards are ending theirs.'

'Actually,' objected his friend, stopping to look back, 'he wasn't drunk. Look how sharply he stopped.'

They studied the tyre marks. 'No, no, no . . . you're joking . . . no, a car like that,' came back Tommaso, 'do it myself! Don't you realize that a car like that stops you dead . . .'

He didn't finish his sentence; looking down at the ground, their eyes had come to rest on a point just off the road. There was something sparkling on a bush. Simultaneously, softly they both exclaimed: 'Oh!'

They got down from their saddles and stood their

bikes against the kerb. 'The chicken's laid an egg,' said Pietro and jumped down into the meadow with a lightness you wouldn't have expected in him. On the bush was a necklace of four strings of pearls.

The two workers stretched out their hands and, delicately, as though picking a flower, plucked the necklace from its branch. They both held it, with both hands, feeling the pearls with their fingertips, but ever so carefully, and as they did so lifted it closer and closer to their eyes.

Then, both together, as though rebelling against the awe and fascination the object inspired, they dropped their fists, but neither one of them let go of the necklace. Feeling somebody would have to say something, Pietro breathed out and commented, 'See the sort of ties that are in fashion these days . . .'

'It's fake!' Tommaso immediately shouted in one ear, as if he'd been bursting to say it for the last few minutes, indeed as if it had been his first thought the moment he'd set eyes on the necklace and had only been waiting for some sign of gloating from his friend to be able to hit back at him with this remark.

Pietro raised the hand that held the necklace, thus lifting Tommaso's arm too. 'What do you know?'

'I know that you'd better believe what I'm telling you: they always keep their real jewels in the safe.'

Their big, tough, wrinkled hands felt the necklace, turning their fingers between one string and the next, slipping their nails into the spaces between the pearls. The pearls filtered a soft light, like dewdrops on spiders' webs, a wintery, morning light that hardly convinces you of the existence of things.

'Real or fake . . .' Pietro said, 'I, as it happens . . .' and he was trying to provoke a hostile attitude towards whatever he was about to say.

Tommaso, who wanted to be the first to take the conversation that way, realized that Pietro had got in before him and tried to regain the upper hand by showing that he'd already been developing his own train of thought for some time.

'Oh, I pity you,' he said, with an air of irritation. 'The first thing I . . .'

It was clear that they both wanted to express the same opinion, yet were looking daggers at each other. They both shouted, in unison and as fast as they could: 'Give it back!' Pietro raising his chin with the solemnity of one uttering a verdict, Tommaso red-faced and wide-eyed as if all his energy were engaged in getting the words out before his friend.

But the gesture had excited them and aroused their pride; apparently good friends all of a sudden, they exchanged satisfied glances.

'We won't dirty our hands!' Tommaso shouted. 'Not us!'

'Right!' laughed Pietro. 'We'll give them a lesson in dignity, we will.'

'We,' Tommaso proclaimed, 'will never hoard their trash!'

'Right! We're poor,' Pietro said, 'but more gentlemen than they are!'

'And you know what else we're going to do?' Tommaso's face lit up, happy to have finally gone one better than Pietro. 'We won't accept their reward!'

They looked at the necklace again; it was still there, hanging from their hands.

'You didn't get the licence number of the car, did you?' asked Pietro.

'No, why? Did you?'

'Who would have thought?'

'So, what to do?'

'Right, a fine mess.'

Then, in unison, as if their hostility had suddenly flared up again: 'The Lost Property Office. We'll take it there.'

The fog was lifting; no longer a mere shadow, the factory turned out to be coloured a deceptive pink.

'What time do you think it is?' asked Pietro. 'I'm afraid we'll be clocking in late.'

'We'll be fined,' said Tommaso. 'The same old story: those folks live it up and we pay up!'

They had both lifted their hands together with the necklace that kept them together like handcuffed prisoners. They weighed it in their palms as if both about to say: 'Well, I'll let you look after it.' But neither of them did; each had the highest possible opinion of the other, but they were too used to arguing for either to concede a point to the other.

They must get back on their bikes again fast, and still they hadn't tackled the question: which of them was to keep the necklace before they could hand it back or in any event take a decision as to what to do? They went on standing there without saying a word, looking at the necklace as if it might somehow answer the question itself. And it did: whether in the skirmish or when it fell, the hook that held together the four strings of pearls had been damaged. A tiny twist and it snapped.

Pietro took two strings and Tommaso the other two, with the understanding that whatever was to be done with them would be agreed on together first. They gathered the precious things up, hid them away, got back on their bikes, silently, without looking at each other, and resumed their squeaky pedalling towards the factory under a sky of gathering white clouds and rising black smoke.

They'd hardly got going before a man appeared from behind a billboard at the side of the road. He was scrawny, lanky and badly dressed; he had been watching the two workers from a distance for some minutes. His name was Fiorenzo, he was unemployed, and he spent his time looking through dumps in the suburbs in search of anything usable. It's an occupational hazard of people like this that they always nurse a stubborn yearning that one day they will discover treasure. On his regular morning round of these fields, Fiorenzo had seen the car set off and the workers run down the embankment to pick something up. And immediately he realized that he had missed a rare, even a once-in-a-lifetime opportunity by less than a minute.

Tommaso was a member of the internal commission that was supposed to see Dr Starna. Deaf and stubborn he might be, with obsolete attitudes and a spirit of contradiction, but still Tommaso always managed to get elected in internal factory votes. He was one of the oldest workers in the company, everybody knew him, he was a symbol; and even though his workmates on the commission had long felt that it would be better to have a more able negotiator in his place, somebody sharper and better informed, all the same they recognized that Tommaso had the advantage of a prestige that came of tradition, and they respected him for it and would repeat the most important things said at the meeting in the ear without the whistle.

The day before, one of Tommaso's sisters who lived in the country and who sometimes came to see him had brought him a rabbit for his birthday, even though his birthday had been a month ago. A dead rabbit, of course, to be casseroled at once. It would have been nice to have kept it for Sunday lunch to have with the whole family round the table; but perhaps the rabbit would go off, so Tommaso's daughters immediately steamed it and he was carrying his share to work with him in a stick of bread.

Whatever they were having for lunch – tripe, stock-fish, or omelette – Tommaso's daughters (he was a widower) would cut a big stick of bread in two and squash the food in the middle; he put the bread in his bag, hung the bag on his bike and set off in the early morning for his day's work. But though this loaf stuffed with rabbit should have been the consolation for a wor-risome day, Tommaso never managed to take so much as a bite of it. Changing for the meeting and not know-ing where to hide the stupid necklace, he had had the bad idea of stuffing it in the bread inside the steamed rabbit meat.

At eleven o'clock someone comes to tell Tommaso, along with Fantino, Criscuolo, Zappo, Ortica and all the others, that Dr Starna has agreed to the meeting and is waiting for them. They wash and change as fast as they can and then go up in the lift. On the fifth floor they wait and wait: comes the lunchbreak and still Dr Starna hasn't seen them. Finally the secretary, a blonde with the beautiful body and ugly face of a cycling champion, appears to tell them that the doctor can't see them for the moment, they should go back to the factory floor with the others and as soon as he's free he'll call them.

In the canteen, all their workmates were waiting with bated breath: 'So? So, what happened?' But union talk was forbidden in the canteen. 'Nothing, we're going back in the afternoon.' And already it was time to return to work: the men on the committee sat down at the zinc tables to grab a quick bite and get back, because every minute they were late would be docked from their pay. 'But what are we going to do about tomorrow?' the others asked, leaving the canteen. 'As soon as we've had the meeting, we'll tell you and we can decide what to do.'

Tommaso reached in his bag and pulled out a head of boiled cauliflower, a fork and a tiny bottle of oil. He poured a little oil on to an aluminium plate and ate the cauliflower with one hand while the other was in his jacket pocket stroking that fat sandwich full of meat and pearls that he couldn't pull out because of his workmates. And with a sudden greedy hunger for the rabbit, he cursed the pearls that were keeping him chained to a diet of cauliflower all day, and preventing him from feeling at ease with his friends, imposing a secret on him that, just at the moment, was no more than an irritation.

Suddenly, standing opposite him on the other side of the table, he saw Pietro, come to say hello before going back to work. The big man stood in front of him twisting a toothpick in his mouth and closing one eye in an exaggerated wink. Seeing him there, well fed and fancy free – or so it seemed to Tommaso – while he was swallowing forkfuls of boiled and quite insubstantial cauliflower, the older man went into such a rage that the aluminium plate started to rattle on the zinc table as though there were spirits about. Pietro shrugged his shoulders and left. By now the last workers were likewise hurrying out of the canteen, and Tommaso, greasy lips sucking on a soda bottle full of wine, dashed off too.

The workers' reaction to the Great Dane when it came into the director's waiting room – they had all turned to the door with a start thinking it was Dr Gigi Starna at last – was, on the part of some, welcoming, on the part of others, hostile. The former saw the dog as a fellow creature, a strong free thing kept prisoner here, a companion in servitude, the latter as merely a lost soul of the ruling class, a tool or accessory, a luxury. The same contrasting attitudes, in short, that workers sometimes manifest with regard to intellectuals.

Guderian's reaction to the workers, on the other hand, was one of reserve and indifference, both to those who said: 'Beauty! Come here! Give us a paw!' and those who said 'Off, scat!' With just a hint of combativeness in the way he sniffed lightly here and there and wagged his tail slowly and evenly, the dog began to do the rounds of the company: the freckled, curly-headed Ortica – the one who knew everything about everything, who was barely in the waiting room before he had his elbows planted on the table and was browsing through some ad magazines left there, and who, on seeing the dog had looked him up and down and said everything there was to be said about his breed age teeth fur – wasn't deigned so much as a glance, nor was the baby-faced Criscuolo, who, his gaze lost in the distance as he sucked on a dead cigarette, made as if to kick the animal. Fantino, who had pulled his crumpled paper from his pocket, a paper forbidden in the factory (he felt himself protected here by a sort of diplomatic immunity and so was taking advantage of the wait to read the thing, because when he got home in the evenings he immediately fell asleep) saw the dog's smoky snout with its glinting red eyes appear above one shoulder and instinctively, though he didn't often let things frighten him, folded over a page to hide the name of his paper. When he got to Tommaso, Guderian stopped, went down on his back paws and sat there with ears pricked and nose raised.

Although not the kind to start playing with pets or people, Tommaso, perhaps responding to a certain awe on finding himself in this brightly authoritative environment, felt the need to offer a few bland overtures, such as a click of the tongue, or a soft whistle, which, in his deafman's inability to control it, immediately came out as extremely shrill. In short, he tried to reassert that spontaneous trust between man and dog reminiscent of his farmboy's youth, of rustic animals, meek droopy-eared bloodhounds or hairy snarling barnyard mongrels. But the social gulf between the dogs of his past and this one, so glossy and well clipped, so much his master's creature, was immediately obvious to him, and intimidating. Sitting with his hands on his knees, he moved his head in little sideways jerks, his mouth open, as if silently barking, urging the dog to make up its mind and shove off, get lost. But Guderian sat still, at once motionless and panting, until at last he stretched out his snout towards a flap of the old man's jacket.

'You've got a friend in the management, Tommaso, and you never told us!' his friends joked.

But Tommaso went pale: he had just that moment

realized it was the smell of casseroled rabbit the dog had caught.

Guderian went on the attack. He put a paw on Tommaso's chest, almost knocking him over in his chair, then licked his face, smothering it in saliva; to get rid of him the old man made as if to throw a stone, as if to shoot at a thrush, as if to jump a ditch, but the dog didn't understand his mime or wasn't taken in, and wouldn't get off him; on the contrary, apparently seized by a sudden enthusiasm, he jumped up raising his front paws right above the worker's shoulders, all the time looking to push his nose in the direction of that jacket pocket.

'Off, boy, come on, off! Come on, boy, God damn!' Tommaso spoke under his breath, his eyes bloodshot, and in the middle of its demonstrations of affection the dog felt a sharp kick in one side. The animal threw itself at the man, baring its teeth at head height, then suddenly snapped at the flap of jacket and tugged. Tommaso just managed to get the bread out before the dog could rip off his pocket.

'Oh, a sandwich!' his friends said. 'Very smart, he keeps his dinner in his pocket, obvious the dogs go after him! Wish you gave us your leftovers!'

Raising his short arm as high as he could, Tommaso was trying to save the bread from the assaults of the

Great Dane. 'Oh, let him have it! You'll never take it off him now! Let him have it!' his friends said.

'Pass! Pass to me! Why don't you pass?' Criscuolo was saying, clapping his hands, ready to catch the thing in flight like a basketball player.

But Tommaso didn't pass. Guderian jumped even higher than before and went to lie down in a corner with the sandwich between his teeth.

'Let him have it, Tommaso, what do you think you're going to do now? He'll bite you!' his friends said, but crouching down beside the Great Dane the old man seemed to be trying to talk to him.

'What do you want now?' his friend asked. 'To get a half-eaten sandwich back?' but at that moment the door opened and the secretary reappeared: 'Would you like to come through now?' and everybody hurried to follow her.

Tommaso got up to go after them, though he was still far from resigned to losing the necklace like this. He tried to get the dog to come in with him, then thought that having the thing appear in front of Dr Starna with the necklace in his mouth would be worse, and struggling to twist his angry face into a smile as grotesque as it was pointless, he bent down again to whisper: 'Come on, here boy, here you wretched beast!'

The door had closed again. There was no one left in the waiting room. The dog carried his prey into a secluded corner, behind an armchair. Tommaso wrung his hands, though what really upset him was not so much the loss of the necklace (hadn't he insisted throughout that it meant nothing to him?) as his having to feel guilty towards Pietro, having to tell him how it had happened, having to justify himself . . . and then the fact that he didn't know how to get out of here, that he was wasting time in a situation at once completely stupid and inexplicable to his friends . . .

'I'll snatch it off him!' he decided. 'If he bites me, I'll ask for damages.' And he got down on all fours beside the dog behind the armchair, then stretched out a hand to the animal's mouth. But the dog, being extremely well fed and trained, what's more, after his master's school of procrastination, wasn't eating the bread, but just nibbling at one side of it, nor did the animal react with that blind ferocity typical of the carnivore whose food you are trying to steal; no, he was playing with it, displaying certain decidedly feline traits that in such a bull of a beast could only amount to a serious sign of decadence.

The others in the committee hadn't noticed that Tommaso hadn't followed them. Fantino was presenting their case, and, having reached the point where he was saying: '. . . And there are men here amongst us with white hair who have given the company more than thirty years of their lives . . .' he meant to point to Tommaso, and first he pointed right, then left, and everybody realized that Tommaso wasn't there. Had he been taken ill? Criscuolo turned and tiptoed out to look for him in the waiting room. But saw no one: 'He must have felt tired, poor old guy,' he thought, 'he must have gone home. Never mind! He's deaf anyway! Could have told us though!' And he went back into the committee, never thinking to look behind the armchair.

Curled up together back there, the old man and the dog were playing; Tommaso with tears in his eyes and Guderian baring his teeth in a doggy laugh. Tommaso's obstinacy was not unfounded: he was convinced that Guderian was stupid and that it would be shameful to give up. He was right. Taking advantage of the animal's feline friendliness, he managed to knock the bread in such a way that the top part flew off, at which the dog leapt off after the half-sandwich he had lost, allowing Tommaso to hold on to the other half with the pearls and the rabbit. He grabbed the necklace, brushed off the pieces of rabbit caught between the pearls, stuffed it in his pocket and stuffed the meat in his mouth, having rapidly reflected that the dog's teeth had never got further than the edge of the sandwich and never penetrated the filling.

Then, treading on tiptoe, face purple and mouth full, the whistle singing high and fierce in his ear, he went through to Dr Starna's office and joined his friends, who all threw him sidelong questioning glances. Gigi Starna, who throughout Fantino's presentation hadn't lifted his eyes from the report spread out on his desk before him, as though concentrating on the figures there, heard a noise as if of someone eating close by. Looking up he saw an extra face in front of him, one he hadn't seen before: a wrinkled, livid face, with two yellow veiny staring eyeballs, and an expression at once furious and blind around cheeks that moved in an insistent chewing motion with an angry noise of chomping jaws. The sight so unsettled him that he lowered his eyes to his figures and didn't dare look up again, and he couldn't understand how on earth that man could have come to be eating here in his presence, and he tried to get the fellow out of his mind so as to be ready to counter Fantino's arguments cleverly and forcefully, but already he was aware that much of his confidence had gone.

Every night before going to bed, Signora Umberta anointed her face with vitaminized cucumber cream. The fact that after a night on the town she had collapsed in her bed that morning – she couldn't quite remember how – without her cucumber cream, her massages and her anti-tummy-flab exercises, without, in short, her whole daily ritual for keeping beautiful, could not but result in a troubled sleep. And it was to her neglect of these rites, and not to the amount of alcohol she had drunk that she attributed the nervousness, headache, and sour taste in the mouth that afflicted her few poor hours of sleep. Only her habit of sleeping on her back, in observation of a beautician's rule that had become a way of life, allowed the restlessness of her repose to express itself in shapes at once harmonious and – she was very much alive to the fact – always attractive to an imaginary observer, appearing as they did between the crumpled folds of her sheets.

Amid her morning bleariness and disquiet, her apprehension of having forgotten something, she was seized by a vague sense of alarm. So then, she had come home, she had tossed the foxfur gown on the armchair, she had slipped off her evening dress . . . but amongst the gaps in her memory what was bothering her was: the necklace, that necklace she should have held more precious than her own soft, smooth skin, she just couldn't remember taking it off, and still less tucking it away in the secret drawer in her toilette.

She got out of bed in a swirl of sheets, fine muslin skirts and rumpled hair, crossed the room, took a quick glance at the chest of drawers, the dresser, wherever she might have left the necklace. She looked at herself a moment in the mirror, frowning her disapproval at the haggard face she found, opened a couple of drawers, looked in the mirror again in the hope that her first impression might have been wrong, went into the bathroom and looked over the shelves, put on a bed-jacket, checked how she looked in it in the mirror over the sink, then in the big mirror beyond, opened the secret drawer, closed it again, pushed a hand through her hair, carelessly at first, then with a certain pleasure. She had lost the necklace with the four strings of pearls. She went to the telephone.

'Could I speak to the Architect . . . Enrico, yes, I'm up . . . Yes, I'm fine, but listen, the necklace, the pearl necklace . . . I had it when we left the place, I'm sure I had it . . . No, no, I can't find it now . . . I don't know . . . Of course I've looked everywhere . . . Don't you remember?'

Enrico, late for work, dog-tired (he'd slept two hours), irritated, bored, his young draughtsman using the excuse of tidying up a project to listen in on every word, smoke from his cigarette smarting in his eyes, said: 'So, you get him to buy you another . . .'

In response the receiver came out with such a shriek that even the draughtsman started. 'Are you cra-a-zy! It's the one my husband had forbidden me to wear! Don't you understa-a-and! It's the one that cost . . . no,

I can't say it on the pho-o-one! Stop being stu-u-upid! If he even found out I'd been wearing it around he'd kick me out of house. If he finds I've lost it . . . he'll kill me!'

'Probably in the car,' said Enrico and in a twinkling she relaxed.

'You think so?'

'I do.'

'But do you remember if I had it? . . . You remember we got out of the car somewhere . . . where was that?'

'How should I know . . .' said Enrico, passing a hand over his face, recalling with great weariness the moment when she had run off amongst the bushes, and they had had a bit of a tussle, and it came to him the necklace could perfectly well have fallen off there, so that already he was experiencing the tedium of having to go and look for it, to search that stretch of scrub inch by inch. He felt a prick of nausea. 'Don't worry: it's so big, it'll turn up . . . Look in the car . . . Can you trust the man in the garage?' (The car was hers. Likewise the garage.)

'Sure. Leone's been with us for years and years.'

'So phone him right away and tell him to look.'

'What if it's not there?'

'Phone me back. I'll go and look where we got out.'

'You're so sweet.'

'Right.'

He hung up. The necklace. He pulled a face. God

only knew what a fortune it was worth. And when Umberta's husband was unable to meet his debts. Very nice. Yes, this could lead to something very nice indeed. On a sheet of paper he drew a necklace with four strings of pearls, filling it in minutely pearl by pearl. He must keep his eyes open. He turned the pearls in the drawing into eyes, each with its own iris, pupil, lashes. There was no time to lose. He must go and search those fields. Why wasn't Umberta phoning back at once? The hell it was in the car. 'You can get on with that on your own,' he said to the draughtsman. 'I've got to go out again.'

'Are you going to see the contractor? Remember those papers . . .'

'No, no, I'm going to the country. For strawberries.' And with his pencil he filled in the necklace to make a huge strawberry, complete with sepals and stalk. 'See, a strawberry.'

'Always after the women, boss,' the boy said, smirking.

'Dirty so-and-so,' said Enrico. The phone rang. 'As I thought, nothing. Keep calm. I'll go now. Did you warn the man in the garage not to say anything? To him I mean, for God's sake, to what's his name, his majesty! Good. Yes of course I remember where it was . . . I'll phone you . . . bye then, don't worry . . .' He hung up, began to whistle, pulled on his coat, went out, jumped on his scooter.

The city opened up before him like an oyster, like a halcyon sea. When you're young and on the move, and especially when you're driving fast, a town can suddenly open up before you, even a familiar place, a place that's so routine as to have become invisible. It's the thrill of adventure does it: the only youthful thrill this prematurely cynical architect retained.

Yes, going after lost necklaces was turning out to be good fun, not boring as he had at first imagined. Perhaps precisely because he cared so little about the thing. If he found it well and good, and if not, too bad: Umberta's problems were the problems of the rich, where the bigger the figure at stake the less it seems to matter.

And then what could ever really matter to Enrico? Nothing in the whole world. Yet this town he was now racing across, carefree and bold, had once been a kind of fakir's bed for him, with a shriek, a fall, a sharp nail wherever you looked: old buildings, new buildings, cheap housing projects or aristocratic apartments, derelict shells or building site scaffolding, the town had once presented itself as a maze of problems: Style, Function, Society, the Human Dimension, the Property Boom . . . Now he looked with the same self-satisfied sense of historical irony on neoclassical, liberty, and twentieth century alike, while the old unhealthy slums, the new tower blocks, the efficient factories, the frescos of mould on windowless walls were all seen with the objectivity of someone observing natural phenomena. He no longer heard that shrill blast as of trumpets at Jericho which had once followed him on his city walks, proclaiming that he would punish the monstrous urban crimes of the bourgeoisie, that he would destroy and rebuild for a better society. In those days, if a workers' march with its placards and its long tail of men pushing bicycles were to fill the streets towards the police station, Enrico would join in, while above the humble crowd he had the impression there hovered, white and green in a geometric cloud, the image of that Future City he would build for them.

He'd been a revolutionary then, Enrico had, waiting for the proletariat to take over and give him the job of building the City. But the proletarian triumph was slow in coming, and then the masses didn't seem to share Enrico's obsessive passion for huge bare walls and flat roofs. So the young architect embarked on that bitter and dangerous season when the flag of every enthusiasm is lowered. His rigorous sense of style found another outlet: seaside villas, which he designed for philistine millionaires unworthy of the honour. This too was a battle: outflanking the enemy, attacking from within. To reinforce his positions he would strive to become a fashionable architect; Enrico had to start taking the problem of 'career advancement' seriously: what was he doing still riding around on a scooter? By now the only thing he was interested in was getting hold of profitable work, of whatever kind. His designs for the City of the Future gathered dust in the corners of his studio and every now and then, while hunting about for a piece of drawing paper, he would find one of those old rolls in his hand and on the back sketch out the first outline of a roof extension.

Driving through the suburbs on his scooter that morning did not prompt Enrico to return to youthful reflections on the squalor of workers' housing projects. Instead, like a deer after fresh grass, his nose picked up the scent of potential building sites.

Indeed it was a potential site he had been meaning to go and see early that morning when he got into Umberta's car. They were coming out of a party, she was drunk and didn't want to go home. Take me to this place, take me to that. For his part Enrico had been toying with the idea for some time: and since they were driving here there and everywhere they might as well go and take a look at a place he knew; there wouldn't be anybody there at this time of day and he could get a good idea of its potential. It was a piece of property Umberta's husband owned, some land around a factory. Enrico was hoping that with her help he could get the man to give him a contract for something big. It had been on the way to the factory that Umberta had come close to jumping from the moving car. They were arguing; she was pretending to be more drunk than she was. 'And where are you taking me now?' she whined. Enrico said: 'Back to your husband. I'm fed up with you. I'm taking you to see him in his factory. Can't you see that's where we're going!' She half sang something to herself, then opened the door. He braked hard and she jumped out. Which was how she had lost the necklace. Now he had to find it. Easily said . . .

A bushy slope of abandoned land fell away beneath him. He only knew he was in the same place as this morning because the road was dusty and not often used and the tyre marks were still there where he'd braked: aside from that the whole landscape was shapeless; never had the official expression, *terrain vague*, taken on such a precise and subtly disturbing relevance in his mind. Enrico took a few steps this way and that peering between the branches of the bushes at the matted ground beneath: as soon as he set foot on the mean barren earth, insensitive to any footprint, strewn with litter, elusive and indefinable, smeared with a streaky pale light that might have been slug slime, any zest for adventure ebbed, the way a readiness to love shrinks and retreats when met by coldness, or ugliness, or apprehension. He was seized by the nausea that had been coming over him in waves ever since he woke up.

He began his search already convinced that he wouldn't find anything. Perhaps he should have settled on a rigid method first, established the area where Umberta had probably been, divided it into sectors, scoured it inch by inch. But the whole enterprise seemed so pointless and unrewarding that Enrico went on walking about at random, barely bothering to move the twigs. Looking up, he saw a man.

He had his hands in his pockets, in the middle of the field, bushes up to his knees. He must have sneaked up quietly, though where from Enrico couldn't have said. He was lanky and lean, pointy as a stork; he had an old military cap pulled down on his head with balaclava flaps dangling like bloodhound ears, and a jacket, likewise military, its shoulders in tatters. He was standing still, as if waiting for Enrico at some threshold.

The truth is he had been waiting there for quite a few hours: since even before Enrico had realized he would have to come. It was the unemployed Fiorenzo. Having got over his first flush of frustration at seeing those two workers snatch what might well be a treasure from under his nose, he had told himself that the thing to do was to stay put. The game was by no means over yet: if the necklace really was valuable then sooner or later the person who had lost it would come back to look for it; and when treasure was at stake there was always the hope you might grab a bit of it.

Seeing the other man standing there motionless put the architect on the alert again. He stopped, lit a cigarette. He was beginning to take an interest in the story again. He was one of those people, Enrico, who think they have put down foundations in things and ideas, but who really have no other guiding principle in life than their shifting and intricate relationships with others; confronted with the vastness of nature, or the safe world of things, or the order of reasoned thought, they feel lost, recovering their poise only when they get wind of the manoeuvres of a potential enemy or friend; so that for all his plans the architect never actually built anything, either for others or for himself.

Having caught sight of Fiorenzo, Enrico, to get a better idea of what the fellow was up to, went on stooping and searching along a straight line that would take him nearer to the other but not actually to him. After a moment or two, the man also began to move, and in such a way that he would cross Enrico's path.

They stopped a yard or so apart. The out-of-work Fiorenzo had a gaunt, bird-like face, mottled with scraggy beard. It was he who spoke first.

'Looking for something?' he said.

Enrico raised his cigarette to his lips. Fiorenzo smoked his own breath, a small thick cloud in the cold air.

'I was looking . . .' Enrico said vaguely, making a gesture that took in the landscape. He was waiting for the other to declare himself. 'If he's found the necklace,' he thought, 'he'll try to find out how much it's worth.'

'Did you lose it here?' asked Fiorenzo.

Immediately Enrico said: 'What?'

The other waited a moment before saying: 'What you're looking for.'

'How do you know I am looking for anything?' said Enrico quickly. He had been wondering for a moment whether he should be brutally direct and intimidating, as the police were with anybody scruffily dressed, or polite and formal like urbane and egalitarian city folk; in the end he had decided the latter was better suited to that mixture of pressure and readiness to negotiate which he thought should set the tone for their relationship.

The man thought a little, let out another little puff of air, turned and made to leave.

'He thinks he's got the upper hand,' Enrico thought. 'Could he really have found it?' There was no doubt but that the stranger had put himself in the stronger position: it was up to Enrico to make the next move. 'Hey!' he called and offered his pack of cigarettes. The man turned. 'Smoke?' asked Enrico, offering the pack, but without moving. The man came back a few steps, took a cigarette from the pack, and as he pulled it out with his nails snorted something that might even have been a thank-you. Enrico returned the pack to his pocket, pulled out his lighter, tried it, then slowly lit the other man's cigarette.

'You tell me what you're looking for first,' he said, 'and then I'll answer your question.'

'Grass,' the man said, and pointed to a basket laid by the side of the road.

'For rabbits?'

They had climbed back up the slope. The man picked up the basket. 'For us. To eat,' he said and began to walk along the road. Enrico got on his scooter, started up and moved slowly alongside the man.

'So, you come round here looking for grass every morning, do you?' and what he wanted to say was: 'This is your territory in a way, isn't it? Not a leaf falls here without you knowing about it!' But Fiorenzo got in first 'This is common land, everybody comes.'

Clearly he had understood Enrico's game, and whether he had found the necklace or not, he wasn't going to say. Enrico decided to show his hand: 'This morning somebody lost something right there,' he said, stopping the scooter. 'Did you find it?' He left a pause then, expecting the man to ask, 'What?' Which he eventually did, but not before having thought it over a bit: a bit too much.

'A necklace,' Enrico said, with the twisted smile of one referring to something that was hardly important; and at the same time he made a gesture as though stretching something between his hands, a string, a ribbon, a child's little chain. 'It's got sentimental value for us. So you give it to me and I'll pay,' and he made to pull out his wallet.

The unemployed Fiorenzo stretched out a hand, as though to say: 'I haven't got it,' but then was careful not to say so, and with his hand still stretched out said instead: 'That'll be hard work, looking for something in the middle of all this . . . it'll take days. It's a big field. But we can start looking . . .'

Enrico leant on his handlebars again. 'I thought you'd already found it. That's too bad. Not to worry. I'm sorry for you more than me.'

The jobless man tossed away his cigarette stub. 'The name's Fiorenzo,' he said. 'We can come to some arrangement.'

'I'm an architect, Enrico Pré. I was sure we could get down to business.'

'We can come to some arrangement,' Fiorenzo repeated. 'So much every day and then so much on delivery of the missing item, whenever that is.'

Enrico almost whirled round, and even as he moved he didn't know whether he was going to grab the man by the scruff of the neck, or whether he just wanted to test his reactions again. As it turned out, Fiorenzo stopped still without making any move to defend himself, an ironic expression of defiance on his plucked-chicken face. And it seemed impossible to Enrico that the pockets of that skimpy crumpled jacket could hold four strings of pearls; if the man knew something about the necklace, God only knew where he had hidden it.

'And how long do you want to spend, combing that field?' he asked, dropping his respectful tone.

'Who says it's still in the field?' said Fiorenzo.

'If it's not in the field you've got it at home.'

'That's my home,' said the man, and pointed away from the road. 'Come with me.'

Fiorenzo's territory ended where the first scattered apartment blocks of the outskirts turned their backs on each other in foggy fields. And near the border, where the capitals of the most remote countries tend to be situated, was his house. All kinds of historic events and upheavals had combined to create it: the low brick walls, half in ruins, were part of an old army stable, later closed upon the decline of the cavalry; the Turkish toilet and an indelible piece of graffiti were the result of later use as an armoury for the training corps; a barred window was the sinister reminder that the place had been a prison during the civil war; it was to winkle out the last platoon of warriors that they had started that fire that had almost destroyed the place; the floor and the piping belonged to the period when it had been a camp first for the wounded and then for refugees; later a long winter plundering for firewood, roof tiles and bricks had once again demolished the place; until, evicted from their last abode, along came Fiorenzo and family with their beds and boards. He completed the effect by replacing half the roof with an old rolldown shutter found in the vicinity and apparently twisted in some explosion. Thus Fiorenzo, his wife Ines and their four surviving children once again had a home where they could hang pictures of relatives and family allowance slips on the walls and await the birth of their fifthborn with some hope that the child would live.

If one could hardly say that the look of the building was much improved since the day the family moved in, this was because Fiorenzo's genius in inhabiting the place was closer to that of the primitive man huddling up in a cave than the industrious castaway or pioneer who strives to recreate about him something of the civilization he has left behind. Of civilization round about him Fiorenzo had all his heart could desire, but civilization was hostile, forbidden territory to him. After losing his job and having quickly forgotten the meagre skills he had somehow once managed to acquire – those of a copper pipe polisher – his hands made sluggish in a manual job that again had not lasted very long, cut out – from one day to the next and with a whole family dependent on him – from the great circular flow of money, it hadn't taken Fiorenzo long to retrace man's steps back along the course of history, until, having lost the notion that if you need something you build it or grow it or make it, he now cared for nothing but what could be gathered or hunted down.

Fiorenzo now saw the city as a world of which he could not be a part, just as the hunter does not think of becoming the forest, but only of plundering its wildlife, plucking a ripe berry, procuring shelter against the rain. So for Fiorenzo the city's wealth meant the cabbage stalks left lying on the cobbles of district markets after the stalls are taken down; the edible grasses that garnish the suburban tramlines; the public benches that could be sawn up piece by piece for firewood; the lovelorn cats that would intrude on common property at night never to return. A whole city existed for his benefit, a castoff, second- or third-hand city, half buried, excremental, made of worn-out shoes, cigarette stubs, umbrella handles. And even way down at the level of these dust-laden riches there was still a market, with its supply and demand, its speculations, its hoarders. Fiorenzo sold empty bottles, rags and catskins, thus still managing the occasional fleeting peck at the monetary cycle. The most tiring activity, but the most profitable too, was that of the mine prospectors who would dig at the bottom of a steep bank below a factory looking for scrap iron in the industrial waste there, and sometimes in a single day they would unearth kilos and kilos of the stuff at three hundred lire a kilo. It was a city with seasons and harvests all its own: after the elections there were the layers of posters to strip from all the walls with the fierce insistent rasping of an old knife; the children helped too filling sacks of coloured scraps to be weighed by the miserly steelyard of the wastepaper dealers.

On these and other expeditions Fiorenzo was accompanied by his two eldest sons. Having grown up to this life they could imagine no other, and would run wild and voracious about the city's outskirts, akin to the mice they shared their food and games with. Ines on the other hand had developed the mentality of the lioness; she wouldn't budge from the lair where she licked their lastborn, she had lost the homely habit of tidying and cleaning, she pounced greedily on the loot that man and sons brought home, sometimes helping them to make it saleable by unstitching pieces of shoe uppers to be sold for patches to cobblers, or scraping the tobacco from the cigarette stubs; and despite their famished life, she had become fat and squat and, after her fashion, calm. The other world, of stockings and cinema, no longer called to her from hoardings whose images to her mind had completely lost their meaning, had become huge indecipherable enigmas. Day after day, when she dusted the glass of the photograph of herself wearing her bride's white veil beside Fiorenzo on their wedding day, she was no longer sure whether it was herself or her great-grandmother. Rheumatism had led to the habit of lying down all day, even when she had no pain. On her bed in broad daylight in the ramshackle house, her baby beside her, she looked up at a heavy, foggy sky and fell to singing an old tango. Thus Enrico, approaching the hovel, heard singing: he was understanding less and less.

With expert eye he took in the warped tilt of the roof, the irregular angles of the fire-mottled walls. One or two effects would not have been out of place in a seaside villa. He should bear that in mind. He remembered a paper he'd once given at a conference on urban design: It is not from the château that we set out upon our adventure, gentlemen, but from the shack . . .

The Workshop Hen

Adalberto, the security man, had a hen. He was one of a team of security men in a big factory; and he kept this hen in a little courtyard there; the chief of security had given him permission. He would have liked, with time, to have set up a whole hencoop for himself; and he had begun by buying this one hen which they had promised him was a good layer and a quiet creature who would never dare upset the severe industrial atmosphere with any loud clucking. As it turned out he could hardly complain; the hen laid at least one egg a day, and apart from some subdued gurgling might have been entirely mute. To tell the truth the chief of security had only given Adalberto permission to keep the bird in a coop, but since the courtyard, only recently annexed to the purposes of industry, abounded not only in rusty screws but likewise in worms, it had been tacitly accepted that the hen could peck around at will. So it went back and forth reserved and discreet among the workshops, was well known to the men, and, for its freedom and irre-sponsibility, envied.

One day the old turner, Pietro, discovered that the equally old Tommaso, in Quality Control, was coming to the factory with his pockets full of maize. Having never forgotten his peasant origins, Tommaso had imme-diately appreciated the productive capacity of the fowl and linking this appreciation to his desire for revenge for injustices suffered, had embarked upon a stealthy campaign to woo the security man's hen and encourage her to lay her eggs in a box of scraps on the floor by his workbench.

Every time he realized his friend was up to some secret trick, Pietro was annoyed, because it always came as such a surprise to him, and he at once tried to go one better. Ever since they had become prospective relatives (his son had got it into his head to marry Tommaso's daughter), they were always fighting. So he too got hold of some maize, prepared a box using metal scraps from his lathe and in the brief respite the machines he ran allowed him, tried to attract the hen. Hence this game, where what was at stake was not so much the eggs as a question of revenge, was played out more between Pietro and Tom-maso than between themselves and Adalberto, who, poor chap, searched the workers as they arrived and left, rum-maged in bags and pockets and knew nothing.

Pietro worked alone in a corner of the workshop set apart from the rest by a section of wall so as to form a separate room, or 'lounge', with a glass door that looked out on to a courtyard. Until a few years ago there had been two machines and two workers in this room: Pietro and another man. But one day the other man had gone off sick with a hernia, and in the meantime Pietro had had to look after both machines at once. He learned how to regulate his movements accordingly: he would push down the lever of one machine and go to pull out the piece the other had finished. The hernia case was operated, came back, but was assigned to a different team. Pietro was stuck with the two machines for good; indeed, to make it clear that this was not just forgetfulness, a time-and-motion expert was sent to assess the situation and a third machine was added: the man had calculated that between the operations for one machine then the other there were still a few seconds free. Then, in a general overhaul of productivity bonuses, to have some dubious calculation come out, Pietro was obliged to take on a fourth. At sixty and more years old he had had to learn to do four times the work in the same hours, but since his salary was still the same, his life wasn't radically transformed, if one excludes that is the development of chronic bronchitic asthma and the bad habit of falling asleep as soon as he sat down, in whatever place or company. But he was a tough old man and, what's more, full of good spirits, and he was always hoping that major changes were just round the corner.

For eight hours a day, Pietro rotated round the four machines making the same series of movements every time, movements he knew so well now he had managed to shave off every superfluous blip and adjust the rhythm of his asthma to that of his work with perfect precision. Even his eyes moved along trajectories as precise as the stars, since every machine demanded a particular sequence of glances to check that it didn't seize up and lose him his bonus.

After the first half-hour's work Pietro was already tired, the factory noises blended in his eardrums into a single background hum with the combined rhythm of his four machines pulsing above. Thrust forward by this rhythm, he worked on in a near daze until, blessed as the first sight of land to the castaway, he caught the groan of the transmission belts slowing and stopping as a result of a breakdown or for the end of his shift.

But so inexhaustible a quality is man's freedom, that even in these conditions Pietro's mind was able to weave its web from one machine to the other, to flow on unbroken as the thread from the spider's mouth, and in the midst of this geometry of steps gestures glances and reflexes he would sometimes find he was master of himself once again and calm as a country grandfather going out late in the morning to sit under the pergola and stare at the sun and whistle for his dog and keep an eye on his grandchildren swinging on a tree and watch the figs ripen day by day.

Of course, such freedom of thought could only be achieved by following a special technique that had taken time and training: all you had to do, for example, was learn how to break off your flow of thought when your hand had to move the workpiece under the lathe, then pick it up again, almost placing it on the piece as it now proceeded towards the grooving machine, and above all take advantage of the moments you had to walk, since one never thinks so well as when one walks a well-known stretch of road, even if here the road was no more than two steps: one-two, but how many things one could think of in that space: a happy old age, all Sundays in piazzas at political meetings listening hard near the loudspeakers, a job for his unemployed son, and then all at once off with a gaggle of grandchildren fishing on summer evenings, each with his rod on the walls above the river, and a bet on a cycle race to propose to his friend Tommaso, or about the collapse of the government, but something so wild as to knock the big-headedness out of him for a bit – and at the same time glance over at the transmission belt to make sure it wasn't slipping off where it always did by the wheel.

'If in . . . (pull up the lever!) . . . May my son marries that idiot's daughter . . . (slide the piece under the lathe!) we can move out of the big room . . . (and taking two steps) . . . that way when the newly-weds lie in on Sunday morning they'll get the view of the mountains from the window . . . (now push down that lever there!) and me and the old woman can move into the small room . . . (straighten out those pieces!) . . . since who cares if we can only see the gas tank from there,' and, shifting now to another line of thought, as if the idea of the gas tank near his house had brought him back to everyday reality, or perhaps because when the lathe jammed for a second it inspired a more aggressive attitude: 'Ifthelaminatesshopstartsindustrialactionoverpiecework, we can . . . (careful! it's out of line!) . . . join them . . . (careful!) . . . with our cl . . . with our claim (it's gone, damn it!) . . . for higher pay grades for our spe . . . cia . . . liz . . . a . . . tions . . .'

Thus the movement of the machines both conditioned and drove the movement of his thoughts. And little by little, softly and stealthily, his mind adapted itself to the confines of this mechanical mesh, as the slim muscular body of the young Renaissance cavalier adapts to its armour, learns to tense and relax biceps to wake up a sleepy arm, to stretch, to rub an itchy shoulder-blade against the iron backplate, to tighten buttocks, to shift testicles crushed against the saddle, to twitch a big toe away from the others: in the same way Pietro's mind stretched and loosened up inside its prison of nervous tension, automatic gestures, weariness.

For there is no prison that doesn't have its chinks. So even in a system that aims to exploit every last fraction of your time, you discover that with proper organization the moment will come when the marvellous holiday of a few seconds opens up before you and you can even take three steps back and forward, or scratch your stomach, or hum something: 'Pompety pom . . .' and assuming the foreman isn't around to bother you, there'll be time, between one operation and the next, to say a couple of words to a workmate.

So it was that when the hen turned up Pietro was able to go: 'Chucketty chuck chuck . . .' and to make a mental comparison of his own pirouetting between the four machines, big and flat-footed as he was, to the movements of the hen; and he began to drop his trail of maize that, leading to the scrap metal box, was supposed to lure the fowl into laying its egg for him and not for that stooge Adalberto nor for his friend and rival Tommaso.

But neither Pietro's nor Tommaso's nests impressed

the hen. It seemed she laid her eggs at dawn, in Adalberto's coop, before beginning her rounds of the workshops. Both the turner and the quality controller got into the habit of grabbing hold of her and poking her abdomen as soon as they saw her. The hen, tame as a cat by nature, let them, but was always empty.

It should be said that Pietro was no longer on his own with his four machines. That is, the job of running the machines was still entirely his but it had been decided that a certain number of pieces needed a special finishing and a few days ago a worker with a file had joined him and every now and then would take a handful of pieces, carry them to a small bench set up close by and, scrape scrape grind grind, he very calmly filed them down for ten minutes. He gave Pietro no help, on the contrary he was always getting in his way and muddling him up, and it was clear that his real job had nothing to do with the filing. He was already well known in the factory, this worker, and even had a nickname: Giovannino the Stink.

He was scrawny, dark as dark, with thick curly hair, and a snub nose that pulled up his lip with it. Where they had found him nobody knew; what they did know was that the first job he'd been given in the factory, the day they took him on, was that of toilet maintenance man; but the truth was he was supposed to be there

all day listening to people talk and passing things on to
the management. Quite what there was to hear in the
toilets that was so important no one ever really understood; it seems that there being nowhere else in the
factory where one could exchange a few words without
being fired on the spot, two workers from the Internal
Committee, or some other diabolical union invention,
had taken to swapping ideas from one cubicle to
another, pretending they were there to answer nature's
calling. Not that the workers' toilets in a factory are a
quiet place, having as they do no doors or just a low
gate affair leaving head and shoulders visible so that no
one can stop for a smoke, and with the security men
poking their heads in every few minutes to see that no
one stays too long and check whether you're defecating
or just taking it easy, but all the same, compared with
the rest of the factory, the toilets are calm, even com-
fortable places. The fact is that these two men were
eventually accused of engaging in political activity during working hours and fired; so someone must have
told on them and it didn't take long to identify that
someone as Giovannino the Stink as he was henceforth
to be called. He was shut away in there, it was spring,
and all day he heard watery noises, flushing, plopping,
splashing; and he dreamed of open streams and fresh
air. No one talked any more in the toilets. So they moved

him. Unskilled, manipulated by the unwarranted fears of a management forever in a state of alarm, he was assigned first to one team then another, given vague and obviously pointless tasks but with secret instructions to spy on the others; and wherever he went his workmates turned their backs on him in silence, not deigning so much as a glance at the superfluous tasks he muddled over as best he could.

Now he had wound up on the heels of an old worker, deaf and alone. What was he supposed to find out? Was he too at his last assignment before being put out on the street like the victims of his spying? Giovannino the Stink racked his brains for a trail, a suspicion, a clue. The moment was propitious; the whole factory was in turmoil, the workers at boiling point, the management with their hackles up. And for a while Giovannino had been churning over an idea. Every day, around the same time, a hen would come into the workshop. And the turner Pietro would prod at it. He lured it with a few grains of maize, got close to it and put his hand right under it. What on earth could it mean? Was it a system for passing secret messages from one workshop to another? Giovannino was sure of it now. The way Pietro touched the hen it was exactly as if he were looking for something, or slipping something inside its feathers. And one day, when Pietro let go of the bird, Giovannino the Stink followed it. The hen crossed the yard, climbed on a pile of iron girders – Giovannino did a balancing act to follow – dived into a segment of piping – Giovannino crawled after it – crossed another patch of courtyard and went into Quality Control. Here there was another old man who seemed to be waiting for the hen: he was watching for it to appear at the doorway, and as soon as he saw it he dropped his hammer and screwdriver and went to meet it. The hen was on friendly terms with this man too, so much so that she let herself be picked up by the feet and, once again! prodded under the tail. By now Giovannino was sure he had struck gold. 'The message,' he thought, 'is sent every day from Pietro to this fellow here. Tomorrow, as soon as the hen leaves Pietro, I'll have it stopped and searched.'

The next day, having half-heartedly prodded the hen for the nth time and then sadly replaced it on the ground, Pietro saw Giovannino the Stink set down his file and go off almost at a run.

When he raised the alarm, the watchmen on duty gave chase. Surprised in the yard pecking at maggots between bolts strewn in the dust, the hen was taken to the security chief's office.

Adalberto knew nothing as yet. Given that connivance on his part could not be excluded, the operation had been conducted without his being informed. Summoned to

49

head office, no sooner did he see the hen immobilized by two colleagues on the boss's desk than his eyes all but filled with tears. 'What has she done? What's happened? I always kept her shut in her coop!' he began to say, thinking they were blaming him for having let the bird wander about the factory.

But the accusations were far more serious, as he quickly appreciated. The security chief fired off a volley of questions. He was a retired carabiniere inspector and over the ex-carabinieri amongst his security staff he continued to exercise the hierarchical authority typical of the force. Throughout the questioning, more than his love of the hen, more than his hopes to become a chicken breeder, what was uppermost in Adalberto's mind was the fear that he would compromise himself. He came clean, he tried to justify himself for having left the hen free, but when it came to questions about the relationship between the hen and the unions, he didn't dare compromise himself by clearing the bird or excusing it. He withdrew behind a wall of 'I don't know, I've got nothing to do with it,' concerned only that he should in no way be held responsible for the affair.

The security man's good faith was accepted; but, with a lump in his throat and a pang of remorse, he was now looking at a hen that had been abandoned to its destiny.

The inspector ordered that the bird be searched. One of the agents stalled saying it made him feel sick, and after some fierce pecking another withdrew sucking a bleeding finger. In the end the inevitable experts emerged, more than happy to demonstrate their zeal. The oviduct was shown to be free of any messages inimical to the interests of the company, or indeed of any other variety. Expert in the many techniques of war, the inspector insisted that they search under the bird's wings, where the Pigeon-Lover Brigade are wont to conceal their messages in special sealed cartridges. They searched; feathers, down and dirt were strewn across the desk, but nothing was found.

Nonetheless, considered too suspect and treacherous to be innocent, the hen was condemned. In the dingy courtyard two men in black uniforms held it by the claws while a third wrung its neck. The bird let out a last long heart-breaking shriek, then a lugubrious cluck, she who had been so discreet as never to dare cluck for joy. Adalberto hid his face in his hands, his harmless dream of a cackling hencoop buried stillborn. Thus does the machine of oppression ever turn against those who serve it. The owner of the company, concerned that he had to meet a delegation of workers who were protesting against firings, heard the hen's death wail in his office and sensed it boded ill.

a little history

Penguin Modern Classics were launched in 1961, and have been shaping the reading habits of generations ever since.

The list began with distinctive grey spines and evocative pictorial covers – a look that, after various incarnations, continues to influence their current design – and with books that are still considered landmark classics today.

Penguin Modern Classics have caused scandal and political change, inspired great films and broken down barriers, whether social, sexual or the boundaries of language itself. They remain the most provocative, groundbreaking, exciting and revolutionary works of the last 100 years (or so).

In 2011, on the fiftieth anniversary of the Modern Classics, we're publishing fifty Mini Modern Classics: the very best short fiction by writers ranging from Beckett to Conrad, Nabokov to Saki, Updike to Wodehouse. Though they don't take long to read, they'll stay with you long after you turn the final page.

MODERN CLASSICS
www.penguinclassics.com